THE GAME

Peter Millett
Simon Scales

Rigby®

www.Rigby.com
1-800-531-5015

Rigby Focus Forward

This Edition © 2009 Rigby, a Harcourt Education Imprint

Published in 2007 by Nelson Australia Pty Ltd ACN: 058 280 149
A Cengage Learning company

1 2 3 4 5 6 7 8 374 14 13 12 11 10 09 08 07
Printed and bound in China

The Game
ISBN-13   978-1-4190-3723-8
ISBN-10   1-4190-3723-4

THE GAME

Peter Millett
Simon Scales

Contents

Chapter 1

"Get Me Out!"

Brad was asleep at his
computer keyboard.
He was snoring.
"Brad, are you in the game?"
A loud voice came through
Brad's earphones.

"Brad, come in…
It's Michael.
I need your help!"

Slowly Brad opened his eyes.
He looked at the screen.
What was going on?

Michael was on the screen!
"Brad, listen to me," he said.
"You've got to get me
out of the game right now."

Brad looked at Michael.
Why was he on the screen?
What was happening?
He looked down at his keyboard,
where a red light was flashing.

Chapter 2

Run

Brad pushed the red button
on the keyboard.
Suddenly there was a loud noise.

Brad spun around.
He turned upside down
and spun in the air.

Brad was then sucked into
the game.

Brad landed on the ground.
He didn't know what was going on.
How had he ended up here?
He looked around and saw that
he was in the computer game.

"Brad!" shouted Michael.
Michael ran over to Brad.
"Run as fast as you can!"

Suddenly a giant foot landed
on the ground in front of Brad.
A red laser blasted a rock
behind his head.

"Quickly, this way!" shouted Michael.
Michael grabbed Brad's arm.

Chapter 3

Control Tower

The two boys ran into a cave.

The giant foot walked past the cave.

A red laser lit up the ground,

and the cave turned red.

"Don't say a word,"

whispered Michael.

Suddenly the red light went away.
"I think I can get us out of
the game," said Brad.

"How?" asked Michael.

"With this."
Brad held up a disk.
"If I can find the control tower
and put this disk in it,
I can shut down the game."

"Hey, I know where
the control tower is,"
said Michael.

"OK, let's go," said Brad.

Chapter 4

Robot

Michael looked out of the cave.
"Run!" he shouted.
The two boys ran quickly.
"There's the control tower!"
shouted Michael.
"Let's go!" shouted Brad.

Suddenly a giant robot stepped out
from behind a tree.

Brad rolled over on the ground
and ran at the robot.
He jumped onto its back.

The robot swooped
and grabbed at Brad.
It tried to shake him off.

Brad pulled out a pen and jammed it
into the robot's control panel.
The robot started to shake and spin.
Then it fell to the ground.

"Run to the control tower!"
shouted Brad.

Chapter 5

Shut Down

Brad and Michael ran
to the control tower.
Brad put the disk in.
He started to shut down the game.
A red light started flashing.

But suddenly another robot
came out from behind a rock.

"Take my hand!" shouted Brad.

Brad pushed the flashing red light.
Suddenly there was a loud noise.
Brad and Michael spun around.
They turned upside down
and spun in the air.

They landed back in Brad's room.
Brad and Michael looked at
one another.
They couldn't believe what had
just happened.

"Thanks, Brad," said Michael,
still shaking.
"You saved my life."

There was one more thing
Brad had to do.
He quickly shut down his computer.